Frog and Friends

Party at the Pond

Written by Eve Bunting

Illustrated by Josée Masse

To my granddaughter, Keelin Taylor Bunting

—Eve

To my sister Geneviève

—Josée

This book has a reading comprehension level of 2.2 under the ATOS® readability formula.
For information about ATOS please visit www.renlearn.com.
ATOS is a registered trademark of Renaissance Learning, Inc.

Lexile®, Lexile® Framework and the Lexile® logo are trademarks of MetaMetrics, Inc.,
and are registered in the United States and abroad. The trademarks and names of other
companies and products mentioned herein are the property of their respective owners.
Copyright © 2010 MetaMetrics, Inc. All rights reserved.

Sleeping Bear Press™

315 E. Eisenhower Parkway, Ste. 200
Ann Arbor, MI 48108
www.sleepingbearpress.com

Sleeping Bear Press is an imprint of Gale, a part of Cengage Learning.

10 9 8 7 6 5 4 3 2 1

Library of Congress Cataloging-in-Publication Data on file.
case ISBN: 978-1-58536-549-4
pbk ISBN: 978-1-58536-690-3

Printed by China Translation & Printing Services Limited, Guangdong Province, China.
Hardcover 1st printing / Softcover 1st printing.   07/2011

Table of Contents

Frog's Party

Frog liked fall.

He liked it when the leaves from the

trees fell into his pond.

They were like little boats that sailed across the water.

He played "boat races" with his friends. And also with himself.

Sometimes a big leaf would drop and Frog could make a leaf hat.

But the best part of fall was his fall party.

Each year he asked his friends, Raccoon, Rabbit, Squirrel, Possum and her babies, to come. There was food to eat and there were games to play. And each one did a party trick.

This year he also asked Chameleon.

"Why?" Rabbit asked when he told her.

"Chameleon lives by himself. I think he is lonely," Frog said.

"Please do not ask him," Raccoon said. "We like the party the way it is. With just us."

"I do not want to be rude," Frog said.

"But it is *my* party. And I am going to ask

him."

On party day Frog dusted and cleaned.

He gathered nuts and berries and some flies

as a treat for Chameleon. And for himself.

He made a leaf hat for each of his friends.

The party was fun. They all looked
spiffy in their leaf hats. Even Chameleon
wore one. But he was very quiet. He did not
join in the games.

"He is new and he is shy, that is all,"
Frog said.

When it was time for party tricks Raccoon did her juggling act.

Possum did her "swinging-by-her-tail" trick. Her babies held on tight.

Squirrel did his "jump-from-tree-to-tree" trick.

Rabbit did her "hop-skip-and-wiggle" trick.

Frog did his "dive-with-somersault" trick.

"Your turn, Chameleon," Raccoon called.

Chameleon did not look happy. He ran and hid in a pile of leaves.

"You do not have to do a trick," Frog

said kindly. He blinked. "Oh my, Chameleon!

You have turned yellow."

Chameleon ran to another pile of

leaves. He turned red.

Everyone clapped.

"That is such a good trick," Rabbit said.

"How did you do it?" Squirrel asked.

"I do not know. I just did." For the first

time, Chameleon smiled.

The party was wonderful. Everyone helped

with the cleanup. Even Chameleon. Each

time he changed color they stopped to clap.

"It is no big thing. I can do it because I am a chameleon," Chameleon said. "I cannot do the tricks you do."

"We are glad you came," Rabbit said. "Even if you could not do that special trick. We like you. You are nice."

Chameleon smiled his biggest smile of all. "I like you, too."

Raccoon nodded. "I always say that it is good to make new friends."

"You did not say that," Rabbit told her.

"I say it now," Raccoon said.

"Shall we ask little Jumping Mouse to our party next fall?" Frog asked.

"Yes!" they all shouted.

And then they lay on their bellies around the pond.

They made leaf boats from their hats and played boat races till it was time to go home.

Frog Dance

Frog was not a very good dancer.

He liked to dance at night. When there was no one to see.

He danced when he was happy. "Tra-la-la-la-la."

He danced when he was sad. Dancing made him happy again.

He danced when it was wet and rain

dripped from the trees. "Spitter, spatter,

splash. Lovely!"

Frog danced to the moon and the stars

and his shadow danced with him all the

way to sunrise.

One night he saw Rabbit watching him.

"Oh no!" Frog was embarrassed. He

hopped into his pond and dived deep.

Rabbit came to the edge of the still, dark water. "Frog, Frog, come and dance. When I am sad I watch you dance. Your dancing makes me happy again."

"**Garrump, garrump**!" Frog said, diving deeper.

"Frog, Frog, come and dance," Raccoon called. "When I am happy I watch you dance. Your dancing makes me even happier. Tra-la-la-la-la."

"When it is raining I come and watch you dance," Squirrel said. "Spitter, spatter, splash. Lovely!"

"And when you dance to the moon and the stars my babies and I stay up all the way to sunrise," Possum said. "Just watching you is a celebration."

Frog peered over a lily pad. "But I am not a very good dancer."

"No matter. Your dancing is filled with joy so it fills us with joy."

"Really?" Frog came out of the pond. "Maybe you should dance, too. Doing is always better than watching. Come dance with me, everyone."

"We are not very good dancers," everyone said.

"No matter," Frog told them.

They danced to the moon and the stars all the way to sunrise.

And the night around them danced, too.

No Kisses for Frog

Frog did not know what had happened.

He was asleep on his rock and then he was not.

He was hanging in a net. Oh no!

A voice said, "Got you!"

Frog tried to jump out. But a hand

blocked the top of the net.

Two eyes stared in at him.

Frog stared back.

"In case you do not know, I am a girl,"

the voice said.

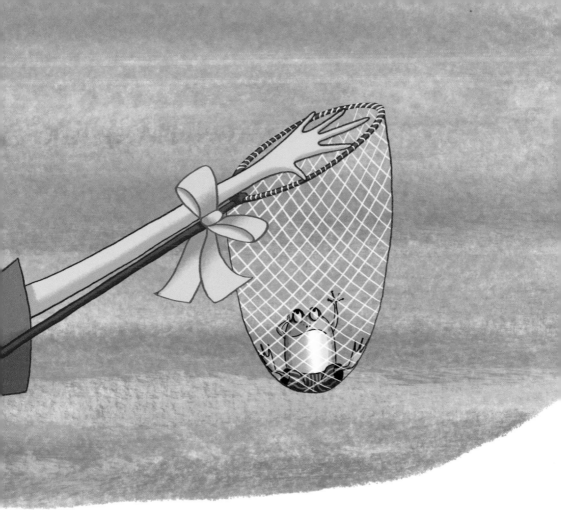

"Let me out!" Frog jumped again and

hit his head. "Ouch!"

"Sorry," the girl said. "I am going to

hold you. And then I am going to kiss you."

"*What?*" Frog was shocked.

"When I kiss you, you will turn into a prince," the girl said. "And you will marry me. And I will be a princess."

"*What?*" Frog was shocked again.

"Hold still!" The girl lifted Frog.

She held him close to her face. They were eyeball-to-eyeball.

"I am sorry you are so ugly," the girl said.

Frog sniffed. "I am sorry you are so rude."

The girl made an O of her lips. Her face came closer. She closed her eyes.

"Wait!" Frog croaked in his bossiest voice. "I do not want to be a prince. I like being a frog. If you make me be a prince, I will not marry you."

She opened her eyes. "Why not?" she asked.

"You would not be happy with me. I shed my skin a few times each year. It is not a pretty sight. Do you want me to show you?"

The girl shuddered. "No. Thank you."

"I like to sleep underwater. Cold, cold water."

"Brr," the girl said.

"I like to have flies and moths for dinner. I catch them on my sticky tongue. See?" Frog flipped out his tongue. A squashed fly, four bumblebee legs, and a half mosquito were still stuck on it since lunch.

"Oh, yuk and double yuk."

"By the way, your hands are too warm. I

am quite uncomfortable," Frog said.

"I am sorry." The girl opened her hands a little. "You will not do those things when you are a prince."

"I will. You could change me outside. But I will always be a frog at heart. What things do girls do?"

"We jump rope. We play soccer. We climb trees."

"I do not think princesses jump rope or play soccer or climb trees. A princess has to wear a crown, and sew, and sit at long dinners. Long, long, long dinners. You will still be a girl at heart. And you will not be happy."

"You are wise," the girl said. "Being a princess sounds boring. I think I will stay a girl."

Frog smiled. "And I will stay a frog. Will you please let me go now?"

"Yes," the girl said. "But first I will kiss you because we are friends."

"Oh no! That might be dangerous. We could shake hands."

"Good."

They shook hands.

She set Frog down and he quickly hopped into his pond. "Come back and see me again," he called. "But no kisses."

He finished off the squashed fly, the four bumblebee legs, and the half mosquito that were left over from lunch. They were delicious.

Then he took a nap.

It was so good to be a frog.